Baby Hugs Bear closed her eyes and tried to n

but she just wasn't sleepy.

She tried to rest quietly but the more she lay still

the more she just wanted to move around.

She sat up, then let herself
fall back onto the bed.

When she landed, she bounced a bit.
"That was fun!" she thought.

Baby Hugs stood up on the bed.
She jumped up a little bit
and bounced off the bed.
"I like this," she said.

Then she hopped...

...and soon she
forgot all about
what Share Bear
had told her
as she bounced
high up in
the air each time.

and she flopped...

Faster and faster
and higher and higher
she bounced.
She giggled with glee.
All at once
she tumbled
too close to the
bedside table

"OW!"

She hit her paw on something
and then there was the sound
of breaking glass.
She crawled to the edge of the bed
and looked down at the floor.

"She will be so angry!
Hadn't she told me
not to jump on the bed?"

"I'm in BIG trouble!"
Baby Hugs sobbed,
as tears came to her eyes.
"What will I tell Share Bear?"

ZZZZZZZZZZZZZZZZZ

Then Baby Hugs
had an idea.
"I'll tell her a stor
about how the vas
got knocked over,"
she thought.

ZZZZZZZZZZZZZ

She tried hard to think of a story.
"I could say that some
star buddies playing tag
flew through the window
and knocked the vase over."

But Baby Hugs Bear thought about how much Share Bear cared about her, and how much she loved Share.

"I can't tell Share Bear a fib," said Baby Hugs.

She went to Share Bear and told her everything that had really happened.

Share Bear was a little upset
about her vase, but then she surprised
Baby Hugs. "When you do something wrong,"
Share began, "it can become a trouble bubble
– it gets Bigger and BIGGER and BIGGER
if you fib or try to hide it."

Baby Hugs Bear helped Share clean up the broken vase, and then took a half-hour nap. But when naptime was over they turned it back into a day **FULL of FUN.**

As Share pushed Baby Hugs high on a swing, she asked, "See any trouble bubbles up there?"